THE DRAGON, THE PHOENIX, AND THE BEAUTIFUL PEARL

A CHINESE DRAGON SPIRIT MYTH

ANITA YASUDA ● JOK

magic wagon

Printed in the United States of America, North Mankato, Minnesota.
102013
012014
 This book contains at least 10% recycled materials.

Adapted Text by Anita Yasuda
Illustrations by Jok
Edited by Stephanie Hedlund and Rochelle Baltzer
Interior Layout by Renée LaViolette

Library of Congress Cataloging-in-Publication Data

Yasuda, Anita.
  The dragon, the phoenix, and the beautiful pearl : a Chinese dragon spirit myth / adapted by Anita Yasuda ; illustrated by Jok.
    pages cm. -- (Short tales Chinese myths)
  ISBN 978-1-62402-030-8
1. Tales--China--Juvenile literature. 2. Mythology, Chinese--Juvenile literature. 3. Dragons--China--Folklore--Juvenile literature. 4. Phoenix (Mythical bird)--Folklore--Juvenile literature. 5. Xi Wang Mu (Taoist deity)--Juvenile literature. I. Jok (Artist) illustrator. II. Title.
  GR335.Y375 2014
  398.20951'0454--dc23
                                                                    2013025309

MYTHICAL CREATURES

DRAGON
Best friend to the phoenix

PHOENIX
Best friend to the dragon

**XI WANG MU
(QUEEN MOTHER OF
THE WEST)**
The goddess of
immortality

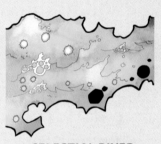

CELESTIAL RIVER
The Milky Way

Note: The Chinese names in this book use the pinyin system to represent the Chinese language in English.

INTRODUCTION

    The Dragon, the Phoenix, and the Beautiful Pearl is an adaptation of the traditional Chinese folktale, *The Bright Pearl*. Its origin is unknown.

    In this version, a dragon and a phoenix find a beautiful stone that they carve into a pearl. The light from the pearl is so bright that it attracts the attention of the goddess Xi Wang Mu. She then wants to own it.

    The goddess Xi Wang Mu is known by many names including Queen Mother of the Western Heavens and Queen Mother of the West. By her palace was said to grow golden peaches that could make a person live forever.

    Many classical Chinese tales feature dragons and phoenixes. They have been an important part of Chinese culture for thousands of years. Along with the tortoise and the unicorn, they were thought to guard one of the four cardinal points: north, south, east, and west.

    In mythology, the dragon and the phoenix symbolized good luck. The dragon was thought to be a gentle creature that brought rain to the people. Later, it represented the emperor. The phoenix's image stood for the empress and symbolized peace.

Once, there was a band of light that lit up the night sky. It was called the Celestial River. Here lived two very special creatures. They were the Golden Phoenix and the Jade Dragon.

The dragon lived in a cave on one side of the river. The phoenix lived on the other side. They saw each other but never spoke.

The phoenix would spread her wings and fly to the stars. The dragon would dive into the icy river. Down, down he would swim to the many colored stones.

Sometimes the dragon would listen to the phoenix's song. And sometimes the phoenix would look down at the dragon.

One day, the phoenix and the dragon saw an island rising from the river.

How fun it would be to explore it, they thought. And this is how they became friends.

When they got there, they found it covered in flowers. This was just one of the island's secrets.

In a pool, the phoenix found something special.
"Look how this stone shines," she said, holding it up for the dragon to see.

The dragon had not seen a stone like this before. "Why don't we make it even more beautiful?" he said.

The dragon held the stone in one of his big claws. Bit by bit, he scratched away at its surface.

"Now, I will use my beak," the phoenix said from her perch in one of the trees. She chipped off tiny pieces of the stone.

Weeks and months went by. The phoenix and the dragon became even better friends. They liked working on the stone together.

When the stone was smooth and round, they looked for water to wash it in. The phoenix gathered dew while the dragon went to the Celestial River. Then they polished the stone until it shone.

"Look," said the phoenix. "It's a pearl!"

The dragon and the phoenix were proud of their pearl. So they decided to stay on the island.

"Together," the dragon said, "we will guard our pearl so it shines forever."

The pearl's magic amazed the dragon and the phoenix. Everything became beautiful in its light. The trees grew taller. The flowers never lost their petals.

"Our pearl is brighter than the sun," the phoenix said.

"Our pearl is brighter than the moon," replied the dragon.

And they were both right. The pearl shone even brighter than all the stars in the night sky.

A pearl this special could not stay secret for long. Far away, the goddess Xi Wang Mu saw its light.

"Is that a new star?" she asked one of her guards.

"No," the guard replied, bowing deeply. "It is a pearl in the Celestial River."

A pearl as fine as this one should be mine, thought the goddess.

Xi Wang Mu couldn't stop thinking about the pearl. With each day that passed, she thought only of how it might be hers. Finally, the goddess sent one of her guards to get it.

"Bring me that pearl!" the goddess demanded.

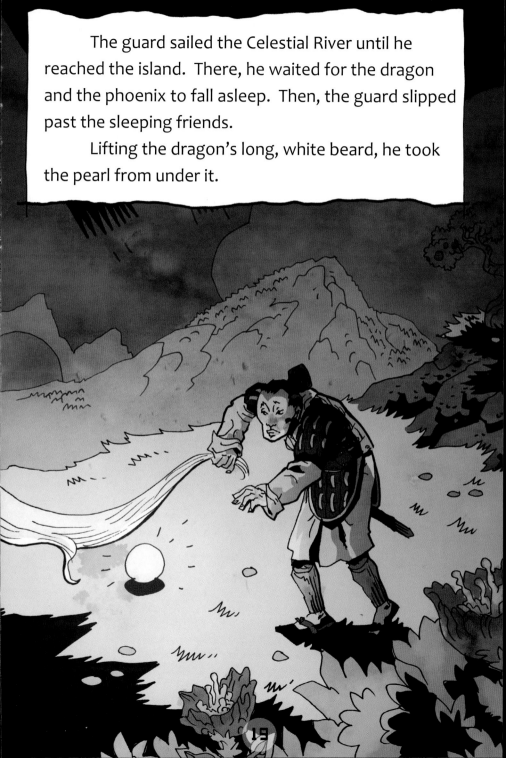

The guard sailed the Celestial River until he reached the island. There, he waited for the dragon and the phoenix to fall asleep. Then, the guard slipped past the sleeping friends.

Lifting the dragon's long, white beard, he took the pearl from under it.

The next morning, the dragon opened one of his red fiery eyes. But no light greeted it. Instead, the dragon and the phoenix found themselves alone.

"Someone has stolen our pearl," cried the dragon.

"Quick," said the phoenix. "There is no time to lose. We must find it."

The friends searched all over the island. The dragon dove into the Celestial River. He looked along the riverbed. The phoenix flew over the treetops. They both could not find it anywhere.

"Don't give up," the dragon told the phoenix. "One day, we will find our pearl."

At her palace surrounded by peach trees, Xi Wang Mu was pleased.

"I have never seen such a beautiful pearl," she said. "And now it's mine."

The goddess hid the pearl deep within her palace. "No one will ever find you in here," she told the pearl. And she closed nine doors behind her.

The pearl stayed locked away for a long time. Though the dragon and the phoenix watched the sky, they never saw its light.

Then one day, it was Xi Wang Mu's birthday party. All the gods and goddesses in heaven came. Xi Wang Mu couldn't help but show off in front of her guests.

"Friends," she said, "I must show you something very special."

One by one, the goddess pulled nine keys from her pocket. And one by one, she unlocked nine doors.

The guests crowded near. *"What could it be?"* they wondered. When the last door opened, light filled the room.

"You will never see such beauty again," the goddess said, placing the pearl on a golden tray.

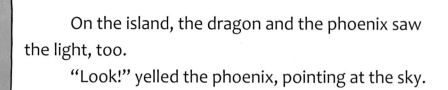

On the island, the dragon and the phoenix saw the light, too.

"Look!" yelled the phoenix, pointing at the sky.

"Our pearl is calling us," said the dragon happily.

The dragon and the phoenix were determined to get their pearl back. They flew higher and higher into the clouds. They followed the light all the way to the palace.

The dragon and the phoenix landed at Xi Wang Mu's palace and ran inside.

"Give us back our pearl," they shouted.

"It's mine," cried the angry goddess. She ordered her guards to throw them out.

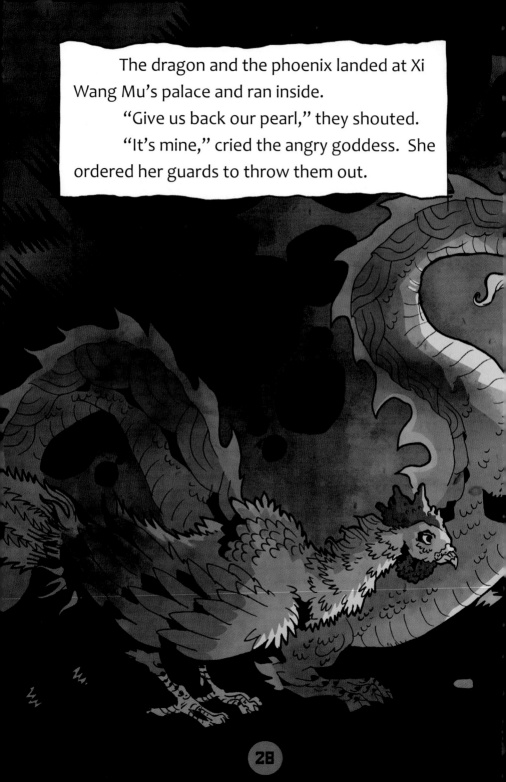

The dragon and the phoenix would not give up. They grabbed for the tray, but Xi Wang Mu was very stubborn. She would not let go. Each pulled with all its might.

In the confusion, the pearl was thrown from the tray. Shocked, the dragon and the phoenix watched as the pearl began to fall.

"Oh no," gasped the phoenix. "We can't lose it again."

The dragon and the phoenix rushed out of the palace. They chased after the pearl as it tumbled toward the earth. Faster and faster they flew, but they could not catch it.

The pearl fell to the island and changed into a shimmering green lake.

"Let us stay here and guard the pearl," the phoenix said.

"Yes," agreed the dragon. "We will be friends forever."

And so the phoenix and the dragon became great mountains beside the lake. To this day they are still there, keeping their pearl safe.